Four Tales
from
Sty-Pen

Brian Leo Lee

Brian Leon Lee

First published in 2016
Copyright © Brian Leo Lee 2016

Cover and Illustrations
Copyright © Brian Leo Lee 2016

ISBN-13: 978-1541254220

About the Author

The author was born in Manchester. On leaving school, a period in accountancy was followed by a teaching career in Primary Education.

He is the writer of several children's short stories including the popular Bouncey the Elf.

A keen Sci-fi reader for more years than he would like to remember, Trimefirst is his first endeavour in this genre.

Now retired and living in South Yorkshire.

By Brian Leo Lee
(Children's stories)
Bouncey the Elf and Friends Bedtime Stories
Just Bouncey
Bouncey the Elf and Friends Meet Again
Bouncey the Elf and Friends Together Again

Mr Tripsy's Trip
Mr Tripsy's Boat Trip

By Brian Leon Lee
Trimefirst
Domain of the Netherworld

All available as eBooks and Paperbacks

www.bounceytheelf.co.uk

For Rita

Contents

VIII

Swerlie-Wherlie's New Friend

Cockie the cockerel began his morning song right on time. The Sun had just begun to creep up over the tall trees at the far end of Farmer Blox's cornfield.

After a full year of practicing his morning chorus, he was ready to give it his best.

'Cock-a-doodle–Dooo! Cock-a-doodle-Dooo!'

'Cock-a-doodle-Dooo! Cock-a-doodle-Dooo!'

'Not now please, not now.'

A small voice whispered tiredly from under a pile of straw, which lay piled up in one corner of the sty-pen.

Swerlie-Wherlie covered his large ears with his little front trotters. It was no use.

Cockie was not to be stopped from giving his morning glory. This was his big chance. Maybe, just maybe, the Poultry Choir Master of the Fowl Club was listening.

There was a vacancy for a lead crower that Cockie knew of. So taking a big, big breath, he really let go.

'COCK-A-DOODLE-DOOOO!'

'That's it,' cried Swerlie-Wherlie angrily. 'A pig can't get a minutes peace on this farm. Cockie has got to go.'

Pushing his way through the straw, climbing over Mumsy and with lots of squeals and oinks from his eleven brothers and sisters, who did not like to be disturbed so early in the morning either, Swerlie-Wherlie managed to get to the sty-pen gate.

'Cockie, Cockie,' he shouted as loud as he could.

Perched on the hood of a large tractor, Cockie paused, just for a moment.

1

Wow! He thought. *Someone at last likes my song.* So he puffed up his chest and began again.

'COCK-A-DOODLE- DOoooooooooooooo.........'

A wet piece of mud had caught Cockie on the side of his head and his song warbled away to nothing.

'Hey,' he called out crossly. 'Who did that?'

As Cockie flipped the mud away with the tip of his wing he saw Swerlie-Wherlie come through the sty-pen gate.

His cockscomb on the top of his head flamed bright red and started to quiver. He was getting mad.

Keep it cool, Cockie – keep it cool, he thought.

'I say, don't you like my morning song Swerlie-Wherlie?'

'Your what,' said Swerlie-Wherlie crossly and he gave a great big yawn.

'Do you know what time it is? We would still be fast asleep but for your screeching.'

'Screeching! Screeching! How dare you. You little pip squeak.'

Cockie jumped up and down on top of the tractor hood and began to flap his wings angrily.

Oh. Oh. Time to go and quick, thought Swerlie-Wherlie and he turned and scampered round the sty-pen and raced away towards the cornfield.

Cockie watched him go and as he calmed down, looked up and blinked rapidly.

The sun was much higher in the sky and he suddenly remembered the Fowl Club Choir.

'COCK-A-DOODLE-DOO.'

'COCK-A-DOODLE- DOOOO.'

He gave it all he had and took a big breath. He had a lot more to do.

Far away, running along the hedges of the cornfield, Swerlie-Wherlie glanced back.

Doesn't he ever stop? he thought, hoping he would.

Dashing down the field was hard work for a young piglet. So he decided to have a rest.

It so happened that in the very corner of the cornfield where he stopped, huffing and puffing to get his breath back, there was a huge tree.

It was a giant to a small piglet like Swerlie-Wherlie and he looked up in wonder at the thick tree trunk and the forest of branches disappearing into the sky. One very large branch was so big and heavy it had bent down back towards the ground. It actually did reach the ground, the end bit making a kind of bridge back to the main trunk.

'Wow! This is just what I need,' said Swerlie-Wherlie as he lay in the shade of the tree.

(It was an old oak but he didn't know that of course.)

There was plenty of dried grass to make a comfy place to rest in and he stretched out his four tired trotters with a big sigh.

'My, that's better.'

What a relief to get away from croaky Cockie, he thought. *No that's not fair, he doesn't croak, he screeches* and Swerlie-Wherlie giggled aloud.

A strange sound made him stop laughing and he looked around the large open space under the giant tree, which was covered by its big branches and leaves.

Then he saw an amazing sight, for a piglet at least.

A small round head had suddenly appeared round the huge tree trunk.

It was just above the ground and it lifted itself over a large tree root which was in its way and a long thin body, dark green on top and with whitish and black blotches along its sides and a yellow band behind the head, slid into view. A pair of golden eyes with large round black pupils stared right at him and a thin blue-black tongue flickered in and out of the mouth.

The shock of seeing a snake, for that was what it was, made Swerlie-Wherlie sit up and get ready to run for his life. Mumsy had warned them, all twelve piglets, never to

go near a snake, as they can bite you and make you ill –
even make you die.

It was the hissing that Swerlie-Wherlie had heard and
then the snake stopped and hissed –

'Hello, who are you? I haven't seen anything like you
before.'

He was unable to say anything for a while. Then he
whispered.

'H.... H.... Hello, I'm a pig and my name is Swerlie-
Wherlie, because of my twirly tail, you know.'

'Hi, Swerlie-Wherlie, my name is Izzzzzabela and I don't
bite because I'm a grass snake.'

The friendly tone made Swerlie-Wherlie feel much better and he relaxed a bit, though he still felt a little nervous as Izzzzzabela slithered closer.

She was about as long as his body when he lay down and as she made a coil of her body, her head was quite high up and he found himself looking at a narrow face with those large eyes, which were peering curiously at him.

Then her tongue flicked out and Swerlie–Wherlie jerked back in alarm.

'Don't worry,' said Izzzzzabela.

'I'm only tasting the air. It helps me know what is around me. That's all.'

'Oh, sorry I was just surprised that's all,' replied Swerlie-Wherlie, pretending that he hadn't been afraid.

'I mean that I haven't met anyone like you before. It was like a sort of shock.'

'Well, to be sure, I haven't met anyone like you before either,' said Izzzzzabela.

'Don't you find it awkward, moving on those four bits sticking out of your body?'

Swerlie-Wherlie laughed. 'You mean my legs? No of course not. I can move on them quite easily. We sort of just do it.'

'Well, I prefer the way we move, nice and close to the ground. We can't be seen very easily and we can hide in most places. So I think our way is best.'

'It sounds good,' agreed Swerlie–Wherlie. 'But we can run fast and jump as well.'

'Maybe, it's the way we are made and so we are good at some things and not so good at others.'

'Yes, I think that's it,' answered Swerlie-Wherlie.

Then he said, 'I don't know about you Izzzzzabela but I'm hungry. Do you know, I haven't had breakfast yet.'

Swaying her head, Izzzzzabela hissed back.

'Now you mention it, I haven't either. Is there anything here you can eat?'

Swerlie-Wherlie looked around.

Of course, he thought.

This is an acorn tree.

'You bet there is,' he said.

His tummy started to rumble at the thought of something to eat.

'All I have to do is root around here. There's bound to be some acorns buried in the soil.'

'How will you do that?' asked Izzzzzabela, looking puzzled at the solid ground.

'With my snout of course.'

And with that Swerlie–Wherlie began to dig the soft earth beneath the tree with his snout (nose).

Within minutes he had found mouthfuls of acorns, which he eagerly scoffed.

Izzzzzabela looked on glumly.

Then she said hopefully, 'There is something around here that I can eat too but we grass snakes cannot get them very often.'

Looking up from his breakfast for a moment, Swerlie–Wherlie asked what it was.

'Those round things you are not eating.'

Izzzzzabela indicated with her head a pile of what are known as galls.

'They have maggots inside them, which we love to eat but the shell is too hard for us to open. We only find a few open now and then. Maybe you can.'

Swerlie–Wherlie thought for a minute and said, 'I know what to do.'

Moving over to the pile of galls, (the larvae of a wasp is inside them) he picked up several with his mouth and gently crunched them.

'Ugh,' He spat out the mouthful of broken gall shells, amongst which were several wriggling maggots.

Izzzzzabela uncoiled and quick as a flash her head had darted down and swallowed the lot.

'Wow that was quick,' said Swerlie–Wherlie and bent down to crunch another mouthful of galls.

'We make good team don't we,' hissed Izzzzzabela in thanks.

'We sure do.' replied Swerlie–Wherlie, grunting with pleasure as he swallowed more acorns.

Sometime later he lay down feeling quite full and happy.

Then Swerlie-Wherlie lazily looked across the open space under the giant tree in which they were now resting after eating their breakfast.

Izzzzzabela was on the far side, taking in the sun, which was shining brightly through a gap in the branches.

Like all snakes, she loved to lie in the sun.

(They actually move much better in the warmth of the sun because they have cold blood. Like all reptiles they need to be warm before they can move quickly).

'I say, what shall we do now. I'm getting a bit bored lying here, though it is nice not to be rushing about, don't you think?'

What looked like a coil of coloured rope stirred and a head lifted up a few centimetres.

'Well, I know a place not too far from here,' answered Izzzzzabela in a sleepy voice.

'A stream goes into a pond and there are all sorts of things we could do there.'

'That sounds good to me. Lets go.'

Swerlie-Wherlie got to his trotters and said, 'Which way is it then?'

'Follow me,' hissed Izzzzzabela and she slithered along quite quickly through the hedgerow behind the giant tree and down a small dyke (ditch) that led to a stream flowing down a small hill.

It was much easier for Swerlie-Wherlie to go down the hill, his short legs had only to keep him balanced.

The stream was moving quite fast. There must have been some rain recently in the area. Small bushes grew alongside it and here and there a big tree with lots of thin branches, which hung right over the water like a curtain. (Though the two new friends wouldn't know what a curtain was and the name of the tree was a willow).

One problem though, was the number of rocks and boulders (much bigger rocks), which lay all around, especially by the banks of the stream. Some were quite wet and covered in moss and lichen.

'I say, Izzzzzabela, can you slow down a bit please,' Swerlie-Wherlie called out.

He was finding it difficult in places to keep up with her.

'I can't wriggle round these rocks like you can.'

'Sorry but we are nearly there now. In fact I can hear the waterfall, so hang on for a few more minutes. Okay?'

It did only take a few more minutes and Swerlie-Wherlie was amazed to see a beautiful sight.

As he rounded a huge boulder he saw the waterfall tumbling down a sort of, what humans would call, a staircase of rocks before splashing into a large pool, which then opened out into a big pond.

'Wow, this is great.'

He was one astonished piglet.

'I've never ever seen anything like this before. It's terrific.'

'Wait until you have been in the water. It gets better and better,' hissed Izzzzzabela, who true to her word, slipped into the pond without making a ripple.

Not to be outdone, Swerlie-Wherlie rushed to the side of the pond and jumped in.

Bad mistake.

He had never ever been in a pond so big and deep before. He began to sink.

'Hey, what's happening to me,' he shouted out in alarm and then he spluttered.

He had swallowed a mouthful of water.

'What can I dooo.....rrrppppp.'

Swerlie-Wherlie's face went underwater again and this time he sank lower into the pond.

Without thinking he paddled madly with his trotters and much to his surprise he rose to the surface of the pond and began to move around.

He was kind of swimming.

Getting over the shock of sinking in the water, Swerlie-Wherlie began to enjoy himself.

He was paddling in a circle when he saw Izzzzzabela not too far away from him.

'Don't you swim,' she hissed, looking puzzled.

'I thought all animals could swim.'

'Well I can't, err couldn't,' he corrected himself as he realized he was actually paddling along as if he had done it all his life. Then he suddenly felt very tired and his legs stopped working. He began to sink again.

'Help. I'm sinking,' he wailed.

In a flash of moving scales, Izzzzzabela had wriggled through the water and wrapped a coil of her body round his front right leg and then slowly but surely wriggled them both to the edge of the pond.

'Phew, that was close,' gasped Swerlie–Wherlie, as he lay, breathing heavily, across a rock that was half in and out of the pool.

It had made a good landing place.

'Thank you. Thank you, Izzzzzabela. You have just saved my life. I don't think I shall ever go in a pond again as long as I live.'

'Well, I can understand that but if you just try and practice near the edge of the pond, I think you could learn to enjoy swimming.'

'No way,' said Swerlie-Wherlie with a big shudder.

'I shall just sit on the side of it and enjoy the view.'

With that, the two, now firm friends, each found a more comfortable place to rest and enjoy the nice warm sunshine. In fact it was so nice and warm they both fell asleep.

A large squeak woke Swerlie-Wherlie and he sat up with a jerk and looked around.

He got a big shock.

Not far away he saw a water vole cowering next to a large rock and there in front of it was Izzzzzabela.

She was coiled up with her head held high. It was swaying to and fro, to and fro. Then she stopped swaying and raised up her head, higher and higher.

'Hey, what are you doing?' shouted Swerlie-Wherlie.

12

Izzzzzabela turned to look at him and the water vole saw its chance and leapt onto the rock and raced away and disappeared down a narrow crack between two boulders.

Irritated at being disturbed and losing her prey, (it was to be her next meal), Izzzzzabela hissed angrily and chased after the water vole.

The crack that it had escaped through was too narrow even for a grass snake, so she slithered back to Swerlie-Wherlie, a little more calmly now. She had realized that he had probably not understood what she had been doing. So she pretended that she had been having a bit of fun with the water vole.

Feeling a bit puzzled at what had just happened, Swerlie-Wherlie said he thought it was time to go back home and since they had met by the giant tree why not go back that way together.

Glad to be friends again, Izzzzzabela agreed.

Puffing and blowing, Swerlie-Wherlie reached the far end of the dyke at the top of the hill.

'Thank goodness we're nearly there,' he said as he saw the giant tree on the other side of the hedgerow.

'I could do with a rest too,' hissed Izzzzzabela.

Then before she could say anything else, with a whoosh, whoosh a large bird came hurtling down and grabbed Izzzzzabela with its talons, before swiftly flying back up into the air.

'Noooo,' cried Swerlie-Wherlie. 'You can't take my friend. Come back. Come back.'

Then he had a horrible thought. Surely that wasn't Barney the owl was it? Barney lived in the farmyard like him, though in the roof of the old barn.

But on the ground where Izzzzzabela had been taken were two feathers, Barn owl feathers.

There was only one thing to do.

Get back to the farmyard as fast as he could.

So he ran by the giant tree and along the side of the cornfield.

He hadn't realized it was so big. It seemed to take him ages to get to the far end of it.

By the time he had reached the field-gate, fortunately not too far from Farmer Blox's farmyard, he was puffing and blowing and his small legs were tired out as well.

Scampering as fast as he could, Swerlie-Wherlie went into the farmyard hoping to see if Barney the owl was there.

Then he heard a scrabbling noise high above him.

It came from the roof of the old barn.

Moving back a bit, Swerlie-Wherlie looked up and saw a strange sight.

Barney the owl was trying to get to his nest through the hole in the old barn roof where a tile had fallen out.

Because he had hold of Izzzzzabela in his talons, he couldn't get in and the more Izzzzzabela wriggled to escape, the harder it was for Barney to enter his nest.

Barney would not give up, even though he was getting tired, for Izzzzzabela was a heavy load for him to carry for a long time.

This had the effect of having to make him dive low to the ground so as to get enough speed before zooming up to the top of the old barn roof and to try to get into his nest.

After watching Barney do this a few times, Swerlie-Wherlie had an idea.

He rushed inside his sty-pen and picked something up before rushing back out into the farmyard.

14

The next time Barney flew down towards the farmyard, Swerlie-Wherlie was ready.

He threw the mud he had picked up in his sty-pen and hit Barney right between the eyes.

Barney, unable to see, flew into the side of the tractor.

He lay dazed, wondering what had happened and where had his dinner gone.

Swerlie-Wherlie rushed over to the little duck pond expecting the worst and was very pleased to see that Izzzzzabela had already got out and had made a coil, not hurt one little bit.

'Thank you very much. Now you have saved my life,' hissed Izzzzzabela.

'That was one good throw. Your sticky out bits can be very useful. I could never have done that.'

'Well,' said Swerlie-Wherlie with a big smile. 'As you said earlier today, we make a good team don't we.'

'We sure do,' hissed Izzzzzabela. Then she said.

'I think I should leave before that owl wakes up and starts looking for me, don't you. It's been nice meeting you Swerlie-Wherlie. I hope we meet again some day.'

'Don't go ......' but she had already disappeared down a hole just by the sty-pen.

Just then Cockie came round the corner of the old barn and saw Barney still with his head buzzing, lying by the tractor.

'Hey you,' he said to Barney in a loud voice.

'Don't you know that this is my practice pitch? Clear off before I make you! Okay.'

With that, Cockie took a big breath and began his practice for the Fowl Club Choir- he hopes.

'COCK-A-DOODLE-DOOOO!'

'Oh no, not again,' said Swerlie-Wherlie and ran as fast as he could to his sty-pen.

****

Swerlie-Wherlie Meets
Sox the Fox

The noise in the sty-pen was so loud it had given Swerlie-Wherlie a headache.

So, getting to his trotters, he shook off a load of straw from his small back and called out, 'Hey you lot, pack it in. Now!'

All of his eleven brothers and sisters stopped arguing and looked over to his corner. They could tell that he was upset.

Swerlie-Wherlie was the youngest of the litter and Mumsy had told all of them that they must look after him at all times. He was so small compared to his brothers and sisters and he often got forgotten about in the crowded sty-pen.

'That's better,' said Swerlie-Wherlie as he pushed through the squabbling piglets and carefully climbed over Mumsy, who was trying to have her afternoon sleep in a shady part of the sty-pen.

Pushing the sty-pen gate open, he turned round and said in a low voice.

'I'm going for a walk to get some peace and quiet. Keep it down so Mumsy can have her nap. Okay.'

Oinky-Oinky, the oldest piglet whispered back.

'We'll try our best.'

As Swerlie-Wherlie walked around the big tractor, careful not to wake Cockie the Cockerel, who was trying to catch up on his lost sleep. He had after all been awake since sun-up. There was a shout from the sty-pen.

'It's my turn you cheat ....'

'Come on,' he said to himself.

'Let's get away from here before I get really annoyed.'

17

The afternoon was sunny and warm, just the weather for a nice walk.

Passing through the cornfield gate, Swerlie-Wherlie went along the hedgerow growing that side of the field, eventually reaching the giant acorn tree in the bottom corner. A hole in the hedge by the tree, allowed him to climb down, then up the side of a dyke, which drained the cornfield. Fortunately, there had been no rain for a few days, so it was dry.

A path by the dyke went down the hill towards a stream that Swerlie-Wherlie had first been shown by his friend Izzzzzabela the grass snake. He hadn't seen her for ages.

He hoped she was all right.

The stream today was really only a trickle of water. This was the chance he had been waiting for. Across the other side of the steam, at this very spot, was a small wood and he could smell hazelnuts.

If there is one thing a piglet likes to eat more than acorns, it is hazelnuts. So, sniffing eagerly, he paddled through the nearly empty stream and entered the small wood.

As he entered a little sunlit glade (a small open grassy space), he heard the sound of crying.

On the far side of the glade by a bush, he saw a small animal. It was a fox cub, and it had been caught in a snare.

Swerlie-Wherlie was shocked at what he saw. Something was pulled tight round the fox cub's neck and it was tied to a piece of wood stuck into the ground.

As the fox cub struggled, the thing round its neck had tightened and the poor animal was choking.

'Keep still.'

Swerlie-Wherlie shouted as he rushed over to help.

18

The fox cub twisted its head painfully and saw him.

'No, don't move,' Swerlie-Wherlie said urgently.

'You will hurt yourself even more.'

The poor fox cub was lying on its side, panting. It had stopped crying when Swerlie-Wherlie arrived and now it watched him with frightened eyes.

He looked carefully at the thing round the fox cub's neck and noticed that it stretched to the stick in the ground.

If I got that stick out of the ground, thought Swerlie-Wherlie, *it would make the thing around the neck looser.*

So, he put his snout (nose), next to the stick and began to root (dig) up the ground.

A pig snout is ready made for digging in the ground and it only took a few moments for him to loosen the soil and the stick fell over.

The fox cub rolled over as the stick became loose and began to breathe much easier.

The thing round the neck was loose as well.

'Wait a minute, wait a minute,' said Swerlie-Wherlie. 'You're not free yet.'

Then he noticed something else.

The thing was actually a thin strap of material which was split and then joined together again by a special link, which, if pressed together, came apart.

By pure chance, Swerlie-Wherlie bit this part and the thing broke in two.

The fox cub sat up, and said in a croaky voice, 'Oooo, thank you. Thank you. I never thought I would get free from that horrible thing. What is it?'

'Well, it's something that some humans make I think. I have heard that some of them don't like us animals and we should keep away from that sort. I'm lucky. I live on

Farmer Blox's farm and he looks after all of us very well. Anyway, I'm Swerlie-Wherlie. Who are you?'

The fox cub rubbed with a paw where the thing had been tight round the neck and groaned.

'That hurts.'

Then the cub looked over at him and said, 'Oh, my name is Sox, because of my two white front paws. No other fox has any like me as far as I know.'

'Hi, nice to meet you Sox. If you could manage it, let's see if we can find something to eat.'

'Well, I could do with a drink first, and then I know just the place. Follow me.'

After a drink from the stream, Sox led Swerlie-Wherlie through the wood until she (for Sox was a fox cub vixen), stopped by a fallen tree.

Swerlie-Wherlie looked around, puzzled.

'I can't see anything to eat here,' he said and he looked around again. 'No, nothing here.'

Sox laughed and jumping up onto the rotting tree trunk, began to scratch the bark.

Her sharp claws, hidden at first like cat claws, soon ripped strips of soft bark away and all sorts of insects appeared, running this way and that way, trying to escape.

Holding her bushy tail high, so that it didn't touch the tree trunk, Sox flicked out her tongue and began to feast on as many insects as she could catch, pausing for a just a moment to say, 'Yummy, yummy. Don't you want some, Swerlie-Wherlie?'

But Swerlie-Wherlie wasn't to be seen. He could smell a hazelnut tree and he wasn't going to miss the chance of a feast of his own.

A while later he came back, walking quite slowly to the

fallen tree, licking his chops. What a feast! No, it had been a banquet. My, how he had gobbled up the hazelnuts. So many, he couldn't have counted them (if he could count of course). In fact he had eaten like a pig and he laughed at the thought.

Sox was sitting on the tree trunk, licking her nose. An insect had nipped her but she didn't mind. That sort of thing sometimes happens when you eat insects.

She looked across to Swerlie-Wherlie as he wandered back, a silly smile on his face.

'Hi, what's so funny?' she asked him.
'Oh, nothing really. I was just thinking.'

And he burst out laughing.

'Oh go on, tell me,' pleaded Sox.

'Well ... I just thought that I had made a pig of myself eating too many hazelnuts. Then of course I realized that I was a pig ....,' and he giggled again.

Sox sat up. 'You silly thing,' she said. Then she saw the joke and laughed loudly as well.

Jumping up, she said. 'Come on, I feel a lot better. Let's go to my place and I can tell my mum what happened to me and how you helped rescue me.'

'There's no need for that,' said Swerlie-Wherlie shyly. 'Anybody would have done what I did.'

'I don't think so and I want you to come. Okay.'

'Well, if you really want me to – all right I will.'

Sox nodded and said, 'I'll race you.'

'Hey, come back,' Swerlie–Wherlie called out.

Too late, Sox had gone. She had run quickly round the fallen tree, then with a loud chuckle, jumped right back over it.

'Come on slow coach,' she teased Swerlie-Wherlie. Then Sox stopped by him.

'Sorry, let's walk together, shall we?'

'You bet,' agreed Swerlie-Wherlie, knowing that his short little legs would not have been able to keep up with her anyway.

They walked along by the stream for a while, and then Sox crouched down and crawled under a thick bush.

'You have to keep your head down Swerlie-Wherlie. We are nearly there.'

Then to his surprise Sox disappeared.

Scrambling along under the bush, it was quite dark and he couldn't see very far.

Then he felt a hole in the ground.

It was a big hole, big enough for him to fall into. He stopped, feeling a bit scared.

'It's all right,' Sox called.

'You can crawl along the burrow and in a minute you will be able to see me.'

Taking a big breath, Swerlie-Wherlie sort of slid into it and crept along in the dark. Then a few moments later, he could see again.

He puffed out his cheeks in relief as he looked around.

Sox was sitting under a small hole in the roof of the burrow, through which a patch of sunlight shone.

Further along it had been widened into a den. Four pairs of eyes glinted in the sunlight as they looked at him curiously.

It was more than big enough for her family (mum and three sisters), to rest in. They were told of Sox's mishap and were so glad that she had been rescued by Swerlie-Wherlie.

'I'm so glad to meet you Swerlie-Wherlie,' said Sox's mum in a quiet voice.

'We shall never forget what you did to save our little Sox.'

'Err. I.... Err, I just did what I thought was right.' Swerlie-Wherlie said, feeling very embarrassed.

'Well thank you again,' she said with a big smile.

'Now, do you like crab apples?'

Swerlie-Wherlie's eyes opened wide.

'You bet I do,' he answered with a big grin.

'Sox, pass your friend some of those in the corner. I'm sure he would like more than one, wouldn't you?' Mum asked, with a twinkle in her eyes.

Swerlie-Wherlie nodded his head so much it nearly fell off.

He actually scoffed several but refused more on the grounds that he was full, thank you. *I shouldn't have had so many hazelnuts,* he thought to himself.

Then Sox's mum told them that she was a little tired. It had been a late night last night, so would they all go out to play and to Swerlie-Wherlie, she added, 'Do come back anytime. You will always be welcome.'

So Swerlie-Wherlie thanked her for the apples and said bye-bye.

Sox and her three sisters rushed out through the burrow leaving Swerlie-Wherlie to find his own way out by himself.

Puffing and blowing, he met up with Sox, who was waiting for him by the big bush.

Her sisters had disappeared.

'Hang on, please. Let me get my breath back,' he gasped.

'You need more exercise,' laughed Sox.

'Come on, you can do it.'

'Its all right for you,' protested Swerlie-Wherlie.

'You're used to crawling along burrows, I'm not.'

'Okay, we'll walk slowly then. Do you mind if we go back to that little wood?'

'Why go back there?' asked Swerlie-Wherlie.

'That's where you got hurt.'

'That's why I need to go back. To see if I'm not scared to do so.'

'Well, if I were you, I wouldn't go back.'

'I have to. Don't you see?'

They walked on in silence for a while and were in sight of the little wood, when Sox said.

'Look, is that a human over there?'

It was and he was doing something strange, thought Swerlie-Wherlie.

He had what humans called a sack and he was pulling something out of it.

'Get down,' whispered Sox urgently.

They both crouched beneath a thick bush.

'He has one of those things I had round my neck'.

She's right, thought Swerlie-Wherlie.

The human was holding a stick, just like the one he had dug up earlier that day.

'What can we do?' whispered Sox.

'Those things will hurt lots of animals.'

Just then a rustling in the bushes made her look round.

'Hello Swerlie-Wherlie, fancy meeting you round here. You are a long way from the farm, aren't you,' hissed Izzzzzabela, the grass snake.

Sox nearly jumped out of her fur when she saw what it was and she bared her tiny teeth.

Then she relaxed when she heard Izzzzzabela say hello to Swerlie-Wherlie.

'Hi, Izzzzzabela, What are you doing round here? I was only thinking about you the other day and when I might see you again.'

'I live near here,' she hissed quietly.

'What's going on and why are you trying to hide?'

'That human over there is trying to harm animals that live round here,' Swerlie-Wherlie said angrily.

'I only just managed to save my friend Sox earlier today.'

'That's right, he did,' Sox said, as she put a paw to her neck and gave a shudder at the memory.

'We have to stop the human from putting more of those horrible things in the ground, and quickly too.'

Swerlie-Wherlie was really worried now.

'Look, he's trying to put one in the ground now.'

'Yes we do but how?' asked Sox.

'Maybe I can help,' hissed Izzzzzabela.

'A friend of mine has a nest near here and there will be other friends with her. I think I can get them to help stop that horrible human from doing any more harm round here.'

Before Swerlie-Wherlie and Sox could say anything, Izzzzzabela had slithered away.

'We can only wait and see what happens,' said Sox.

Swerlie-Wherlie nodded in agreement.

A short time later, there was a loud shout and a scream. They both looked through the bush and saw the human surrounded by snakes.

Lots and lots of them.

'It must be Izzzzzabela and her friends,' shouted Swerlie-Wherlie and he watched as the snakes formed a ring and lifted up their heads, which began to sway, this way and that way, this way and that way.

The human had dropped the sack full of the horrible objects and as he backed away waving his arms and shouting, he stepped into the snare he had just fixed into the ground.

It pulled tight, just above his ankle and he fell to the ground shouting for help but there was nobody else around.

Izzzzzabela hissed a message to her friends and they all began to slither towards the human who was pulling like mad at the stick to get it out of the ground.

Then Izzzzzabela hissed

'Now.'

And all of her friends flicked out their forked tongues.

The human shrank back.

'Go away!' he shouted.

'Go away!'

Then with a huge tug, he pulled the stick out of the ground.

28

He was then able to press the special place on the thin strap and it broke in two.

He was free and as he got to his feet he threw the bits of the broken snare at the nearest snake and ran through a gap in the ring of snakes, which Izzzzzabela had left ready for him to use.

One thing for sure, he was never going to come back here again with his horrible things.

Sox was over the moon and wanted to thank Izzzzzabela and her friends for what they had done but they had all gone before she could do so.

'Don't worry about it,' said Swerlie-Wherlie.

'That's Izzzzzabela all over. She will be back and you will be able to thank her and her friends then.'

'But there is one thing we have to do, Sox. Get rid of all those horrible things.'

'You know this area pretty well don't you, Sox. Is there a place we can hide them? A place not well known.'

Sox thought hard for a few moment and said, 'Yes, I do know of a place and it is not too far from here either.'

So after putting the broken snare, which was still lying where it had been thrown, into the big bag with all the others. Swerlie-Wherlie and Sox, each grabbing a corner of the bag with their teeth, slowly dragged it to the secret place that Sox knew of.

It was a sort of cave, set into the hill, not too far from the stream and inside it was a deep, deep hole, into which they dropped the bag of horrible things.

Tired but happy, Swerlie-Wherlie said, 'Come back to the farm with me and meet my family. I'm sure they will like you Sox.'

'That's nice of you. I would love to meet your family.'

The walk up to the cornfield gate was tiring and Swerlie-Wherlie stopped to have a rest, before going onto the lane which led straight to the farmyard.

Then Swerlie-Wherlie had a sudden thought.

Was he doing the right thing bringing Sox to the farm? The sty-pen was big though wasn't it? It had to be. He had a big family. Then he realized that a lot of it was open to the sky and Sox was used to her den, deep underground. Would she feel safe with all eleven of his brothers and sisters, each one trying to find the best and most comfortable space for themselves, which led to a lot of pushing and squealing.

Then there was the food trough. That caused a lot of pushing too. Maybe he had better find a way of not taking Sox straight to the sty-pen.

Feeling a bit awkward, Swerlie-Wherlie led Sox into the farmyard and it all happened at once.

The clucking of the hens stopped.

The ducks stopped quacking and Cockie the cockerel gave a huge screech and shouted.

'FOX! FOX! Run! Run for your lives!'

He then flew straight to the top of the old barn.

He was so excited at seeing a fox in broad daylight he forgot all about Barney the owl's nest, under a hole made by a loose tile in the old barn's roof.

He lost his balance and fell through it and landed in the middle of the nest right on top of Barney himself, who was fast asleep.

Cockie's luck went from bad to worse.

He had not only woke Barney, he woke the whole brood of owlet chicks, all six of them.

'Hey, what the .....'

A startled Barney suddenly became aware of Cockie lying by the nest and his owlets, now awake, begging for food.

'You idiot!'

Barney was mad.

Everyone in the farmyard knew of his bad temper and always tried to stay away from him when he was upset and he sure was upset now.

Cockie did his best to flap his way from the nest but Barney's fierce voice made him stop.

'You'll pay for this, Cockie, mark my words. Just look at my little darlings. All upset, because of you.'

'Sorry. I'm so sorry Barney. I didn't mean to fall into your nest. It was an accident, honest.'

Then Cockie had an idea that might get him out of trouble.

'I'll make it up to you, Barney. Just say what you want me to do and I'll do it. Promise.'

Barney looked down with his big fierce eyes and Cockie was terrified of what he might do.

Then Barney smiled.

He had thought of something. Cockie had done it big time and now was the time to make him put it right.

'All right Cockie. I'm a reasonable owl,' said Barney.

'Let's say it was an accident but you did wake up all of my darling owlets and that's not good. They could be upset for days. Days I say.'

Cockie cringed, waiting to be told what horrible things he had to do to please Barney.

Barney's big eyes gleamed in the semi-darkness of the old barn roof and then he said in a fierce voice, 'Cockie, you are to feed my owlets for the next week. As many worms as they can eat. Do you understand?'

As Cockie looked on, Barney lifted one of his feet and waved his terribly sharp talons in front of Cockle's face.

'Y ... y ... yes, Barney,' said Cockie in a croaky voice, as he leaned back from the tip of the middle and longest talon.

'I'll do it.'

'Good.'

Barney smiled to himself again.

'Now go and find out what that row in the farmyard is all about, and tell them to keep it quiet. I want to get some sleep. Okay.'

Cockie wiped his face with the tip of his wing,

Phew, he thought. *That wasn't as bad as it might have been.*

'Just as you say Barney, just as you say,' Cockie said, as he climbed up to the hole in the roof and squeezed through it.

By now the hens had run to their hut, safe inside and clucking madly to themselves and the panicky ducks, wings flapping, and quacking loudly, had run under the big tractor, hoping not to be seen.

The Farmhouse door crashed open and Farmer Blox rushed out holding his shotgun.

He had been having a nice cup of tea when the hullabaloo broke out.

He was not happy at being disturbed and the sight of Sox the fox (he didn't notice Swerlie-Wherlie), made him lift up his shotgun and as he rushed forward he got ready to take aim and fire it.

At that very moment, his yard dog Flash, decided to help and raced across the farmyard towards Sox.

The lead for Flash had to be long, so that he could patrol the farmyard and that was the problem.

In his eagerness to get to Sox, he ran by Farmer Blox and the lead got caught between Farmer Blox's feet.

This caused him to fall and as he did so the shotgun fired.

The shot was deafening and a cloud of smoke went high over the sty-pen, making Swerlie-Wherlie and Sox crouch down quickly.

The bang of the shotgun seemed to jolt Swerlie-Wherlie into action.

'Sox. Come with me. We have to get away from here, right now. Come on.'

His urgent voice was enough to make Sox move.

'Where are we going,' she asked. hoping it would be somewhere much quieter.

Across the farmyard, next to a store shed in which worn out tools like scythes, old wagon wheels and machine parts were kept, there was a large heap of hay stacked against the wall.

'Follow me,' whispered Swerlie-Wherlie.

'But keep as low to the ground as you can. It doesn't matter if they can see me.'

In a few moments they had hidden themselves under the hay.

Farmer Blox was still trying to untangle himself from Flash's lead.

It was made much more difficult because Flash, over-excited but enjoying every minute (it was the best thing that had happened to him for ages), kept running round Farmer Blox.

Each time more of his lead wrapped itself tighter and tighter until Farmer Blox fell over again.

'Flash, Flash, give over boy,' he kept on shouting.

'Sit. Sit. Boneos, Boneos, sit Flash. Good boy. Do you want your Boneo now? I said sit Flash, sit.'

Flash gave a loud bark and tried to run to the farmhouse for a Boneo. The lead stopped him, so he turned back and began to whine.

Just then the farmers wife came out.

'For goodness sake, what's going on? My word, why have you got Flash's lead round your feet? And look, your shotgun is in the duck pond. I don't think that will do it any good, do you? Why have you put it in there? I can't believe it and don't stay down there all day either. I'll come back when you've sorted it all out.'

Farmer Blox gave a big sigh and pulled Flash closer. He could now free himself from the tangled lead.

'Home boy, home,' he said to Flash, who by now had calmed down, gave a little yelp and ran back to his kennel.

Feeling stiff all-over Farmer Blox crossed over to the little duck pond and picked up his dripping-wet shotgun.

'More work,' he muttered to himself, thinking of all the oiling and cleaning he would have to do to it tonight.

He plodded back to the farmhouse, all thoughts of catching the fox gone.

Now that things had quietened down Swerlie-Wherlie whispered to Sox, 'Now is our chance. I think I can get you to the cornfield gate without anyone seeing you. Are you ready?'

Sox was more than ready. She wanted to get home as quickly as possible. She didn't like farmyards anymore.

'Yes,' she said quietly.

'Can we go now please.'

So Swerlie–Wherlie grabbed a pile of hay between his trotters and covered Sox with it.

'Now,' he said quietly, 'Walk slowly and we can reach the cornfield gate in no time.'

At the gate, Sox looked at Swerlie–Wherlie for a long time and then said.

'I can never thank you enough for saving me and I hope

we can be friends for ever.'

Sox touched Swerlie-Wherlie gently on the face with a paw.

'Bye and look after yourself.'

'And you,' he called out but she had already gone.

What a day it has been, he thought as he went back through the farmyard.

A scuffle in the corner of the old barn made him stop.

It was Cockie, scratching in the dirt, and instead of eating the big worm he had found, he put it on a big leaf, which seemed to be covered with them.

Cockie looked around carefully to see if anyone was watching. Then he folded the big leaf of worms under a wing and went inside the old barn.

How strange, thought Swerlie-Wherlie as he walked towards the sty-pen.

'That's mine you cheat.....'

A voice was loudly complaining amongst a babble of squeals and grunts.

Then.

'Shsssssssss, you'll wake Mumsy.'

****

Swerlie-Wherlie
and
Bulfrey the Bull

It was so quiet, well not that quiet. Swerlie-Wherlie could just hear the gentle snore of Mumsy who lay in the early morning shade of the sty-pen's high wall.

I must have overslept, he thought to himself as he stretched his four little trotters and looked around the sty-pen.

He sat up with a jerk.

'Hey, where is everybody?'

One of Mumsy's large ears twitched.

Ooops, I'd better not make a noise, he thought. *Mumsy did not like being wakened from one of her many naps.*

Then he looked around again.

Not one of his eleven brothers and sisters were to seen.

It was the lack of their squabbling, the grunts and squeals that Swerlie-Wherlie had noticed. He might have stayed asleep forever.

Careful not to wake Mumsy, he crept through the sty-pen gate and began to cross Farmer Blox's farmyard.

'Hi Swerlie-Wherlie, looks like it's going to be a nice day, don't you think?' A friendly voice said.

Cockie the cockerel had stopped preening his feathers for a moment to look at Swerlie-Wherlie.

He was feeling so much better today. He didn't have to do

any more of what Barney the Barn owl had asked him to do.
Feed his owlets for one week. A whole week!

Asked......

More like told me what to do or else and Cockie shuddered
at the thought of Barney's staring big eyes and those fierce,
long sharp talons and what might have happened if he had
said no.

Then Cockie bent down and gave Swerlie-Wherlie such
a look.

Swerlie-Wherlie just stared at Cockie in amazement.

'Are you okay?' he asked politely.

He knew that the young animals on the farm usually
kept away from Cockie, who often picked on them for
nothing.

Cockie leaned back and stretched his large colourful
wings.

'Couldn't be better, couldn't be better,' he said
cheerfully and to prove it he took a big breath.

'Cockadoodle Doooooo!'

Oh no, thought Swerlie-Wherlie.

"Sorry Cockie, I have to go.'

And he rushed out of the farmyard, past the cornfield
gate and didn't stop until he reached the large meadow.

He paused only long enough to crawl through a small
gap in the hedge by the padlocked gate.

Funny, he thought. *Why is the gate padlocked?*

He entered the field.

On the far side of it he saw a large brown animal lying
down. It turned a huge head, which had a set of long horns
sticking out and looked curiously at him.

He walked slowly over and stopped.

'Hello,' a deep voice said.

'I don't get many visitors these days. It's nice to meet you. I'm Bulfrey the Bull.'

Swerlie-Wherlie looked up at Bulfrey. He felt so small standing next to him.

'Err, I'm Swerlie-Wherlie.'

He was beginning to like Bulfrey, so he asked him if there were any acorn trees near his meadow.

'Just a minute,' said Bulfrey, getting to his feet.

He towered over Swerlie-Wherlie and had to move two or three steps backwards so that he could look down at him.

'You're not very big,' he said.

'I mean you can't be very old.'

'Well I am a piglet.'

'That means I'm very young. You should see my dad though. He's huge. Err, not like you though, Bulfrey. I think you are the biggest bull in the whole world.'

Bulfrey coughed, and pawed the ground with one large front hoof and his long tail flicked to and fro.

'I wouldn't go that far, Swerlie-Wherlie,' he said. Though he was mighty pleased by the compliment.

'Yes, actually there are some acorn trees in the next meadow. Would you like me to show you?'

'If you don't mind, yes please.'

So the pair of them walked slowly along the hedgerow towards a gap that led to the next meadow.

Swerlie-Wherlie was feeling happy.

This was turning out to be an exciting day.

The next field sloped down to a narrow lane along which several acorn trees grew.

A twitch of his nose told Swerlie-Wherlie that there were acorns nearby, lots and lots of them.

'Do you like acorns, Bulfrey?'

Bulfrey gave a loud snort.

'Well I don't, though some cattle do eat them. I have heard that acorns can give cows tummy ache. That's why I don't eat them.'

'Oh goody, more for me.'

'Now now, Swerlie-Wherlie I hope you aren't one of those greedy animals that don't know when to stop eating when they are full?'

'How can you say that, Bulfrey. Me, a little piglet – greedy, I hope not.'

But he said it with a little smile.

While Swerlie-Wherlie was rooting for acorns, Bulfrey was enjoying eating the long grass, which grew alongside the hedgerow.

They were suddenly interrupted by an ewe sheep, which came dashing through the hedge as though she was being chased by a pack of hungry wolves.

'Hey, steady on, slow down. What's the hurry?'

Bulfrey said, hurriedly shifting his huge body out of the way.

Then he gave a big snort of surprise.

'My, it's little Eulia. Why are you running so fast?'

'Oh thank goodness it's you Bulfrey,' panted Eulia.

'Can you help me. Please, please. Can you help me, Bulfrey?'

'What's the matter,' asked Bulfrey kindly.

'Take your time and tell me.'

Eulia looked up at him for a moment and said, 'It's my flock. Some humans have captured them and I think they will take them all away. I only just got away because I went for a drink in the stream.'

Still puffing hard, she lay down under the acorn tree, trying to get her breath back.

It took some time but Eulia eventually felt calm enough to tell them more of what had happened.

Further down the lane, she told them, the fields went up a big hill. There were few hedges, so the flock could graze (eat grass) wherever they wanted.

It didn't matter really, because the flock never went too far away, and their shepherd could easily find them.

Anyway, Eulia went on, *earlier that day, some humans and a sheepdog came up the hill and drove the flock down to the old mill next to a stream.*

That's where I was having my drink when I heard a dog barking. The tall bracken by the stream hid me from the humans and the sheepdog was too busy guiding the flock to notice me.

Then the flock was driven inside the old mill and a big door was closed, trapping them inside.

I was wondering what to do when a human shouted and the sheepdog suddenly looked towards me and barked. I knew I had been seen so I ran in the stream and then back to the lane, keeping as low as I could in the bracken. I came here as fast as I could, hoping to get some help to rescue my friends.

Eulia stopped and stared at Bulfrey hopefully.

Bulfrey looked down at her, she was not much bigger than Swerlie-Wherlie and said, 'I think you were very lucky, Eulia. That sheepdog must have lost your scent when you ran down the stream, otherwise ... well .... errmm.'

He was interrupted by Swerlie-Wherlie.

'Let's go and see what's happening at the old mill. Maybe we can help Eulia rescue her friends.'

Bulfrey wanted to help, but he was so big.

'Surely,' he said carefully, 'I would be seen from a long way off.'

'You would be, but what if you had some of your herd with you. Nobody would think you were doing anything by walking down a lane with them.'

Swerlie-Wherlie was getting excited at the thought of being part of an adventure.

'That might work,' said Bulfrey as he looked over to the other side of the meadow where several cows were grazing.

'It's a start anyway. I'll get my friends from over there.' And he pointed with his huge head towards them.

'Moooooo! Mooooo!' he called loudly.

The cows stopped grazing and looked over the field at Bulfrey.

'Moooooo! Mooooooo!'

He called again and the cows began to slowly walk towards him.

'I think it's better if you two make your own way to the old mill but make sure you're not seen,' Bulfrey said.

'Then we can follow you down the lane as though we are going back to the farm. I can explain to my friends what has happened to Eulia and her flock on the way.'

Swerlie-Wherlie and Eulia both nodded and went to the hole in the hedge by the acorn tree.

Eulia being the oldest went first and carefully pushed through the hedge.

The lane was empty.

It was easier for Swerlie-Wherlie, as he was much smaller and they were soon on their way down the lane.

When they reached the bridge over the stream, Eulia stopped and said, 'This is where I got out of the water. If we go back the same way we might not be seen.'

'Good idea,' said Swerlie-Wherlie.

There was a gap between the hedgerow and the stonewall of the bridge which they got through quite easily and then made their way down the steep side of the stream.

Fortunately, it was not very deep, so they were able to walk carefully upstream without much difficulty.

Another thing Swerlie-Wherlie noticed which helped them were the bushes growing alongside the stream. They gave good cover as they got near the old mill.

'Baaa. Baaa.'

The bleating of lots of sheep was suddenly heard.

'That's my flock,' whispered Eulia quietly.

'They don't sound very happy. I do hope Bulfrey will be able to rescue them.'

'I'm sure he will do his best,' said Swerlie-Wherlie, crossing his tail for luck.

'Shssssss,' hissed Eulia urgently, 'There's the old mill.'

Through a gap in the bushes, Swerlie-Wherlie saw an old building.

It was built on the side of a small hill. The stream had once rushed down the slope next to the old mill but Swerlie-Wherlie noticed that it had changed its direction; the stream bed was now dry, (the water in the stream was now running below the spot where they were hiding, not too far from the mill yard).

The water wheel fixed to the wall had not been used for many, many years. That's why the building had been left empty. Half the roof was gone and all the windows were broken. The only sign that it was being used were the big double doors, firmly shut and padlocked with a shiny new chain.

A rough track went from the mill yard to a small bridge

that crossed the stream that they were standing in and joined the lane that Bulfrey and his friends were coming up. So Swerlie-Wherlie hoped.

A large lorry was parked by the big doors, with dark smelly smoke coming from its exhaust pipe.

'Baaa, Baaa.'

More cries from the old mill.

Just then, Swerlie-Wherlie heard the clumping of heavy feet in the lane. Turning round he saw Bulfrey leading two of his friends as though they hadn't a care in the world.

'Bulfrey,' he whispered as loud as he dared.

'Bulfreyyyyy.'

Fortunately, Bulfrey heard Swerlie-Wherlie and was quite surprised when Swerlie-Wherlie came up to the fence by the side of the lane.

'Hello, Swerlie-Wherlie, I didn't expect to see you so soon. These are my two friends, Daisy and Buttercup. I have told them about Eulia and the missing sheep and they have agreed to help.'

Buttercup and Daisy nodded their heads, as they continued chewing their cud. (A mouthful of grass).

'That's just it, Bulfrey. We don't know what to do yet. Could and your friends sort of have something to eat around here until me and Eulia can think of a plan to save her flock.'

Bulfrey looked around.

He pointed with his nose.

'That seems to be a good place for us to graze. There is a patch of grass just over that bridge.'

'Super, that should give us time to think of something. Thanks Bulfrey,' Swerlie-Wherlie said.

'We'll see you in a bit, okay.'

Bulfrey nodded and led his two friends down towards the bridge.

Swerlie-Wherlie watched them go and crept back to where he had left Eulia.

'What's happening?' she asked anxiously.'

'Err, not a lot at the moment,' he said in a worried voice.

'To be honest, I don't have a clue of what to do next.'

Before Eulia could say anything else, there was a rustling in the bushes and a long thin body appeared.

'Hi, I thought I recognized your voice.'

It was Izzzzzabela, the grass snake and she slithered closer to them.

Eulia had crouched down behind Swerlie-Wherlie when she saw Izzzzzabela, feeling very scared of being so near a snake.

'It's okay, Eulia, this is my friend. She saved me when I was in trouble not long ago, didn't you Izzzzzabela?'

Forming a coil by twisting her body round and round, Izzzzzabela could lift her head quite high and looked at Eulia.

'I only did what a good friend would do,' she hissed. 'Anyway you saved me from that big bird, didn't you?'

Ah, yes, Swerlie–Wherlie remembered.

Barney the owl had caught her, not knowing she was his friend.

'Well then,' said Eulia feeling more relaxed.

'A friend of Swerlie-Wherlie is a friend of mine as well but what are we going to do about my flock?'

Izzzzzabela's head swayed too and fro. She was curious about what Eulia meant.

Swerlie-Wherlie quickly told her about the sheep being taken by the bad humans and how he had asked Bulfrey

49

and his friends to help rescue them.

'The trouble is, I can't think of a way to do it.'

He looked at Izzzzzabela, 'Can you think of something?'

'Well, one thing I can do, is sneak into the building where they are being kept and see if there is a way of getting all of them safely out.'

'Wow, that would be fantastic,' said Swerlie-Wherlie.

'We'll creep down to Bulfrey by the bridge and tell him what you are doing. All right?'

Izzzzzabela nodded her head and slithered off down the banking and crossed the stream, before wriggling between small bushes and clumps of grass towards the old mill as Swerlie-Wherlie and Eulia made their careful way to Bulfrey and his friends.

Snakes can move much faster than most through rough ground and she was soon by the old mill next to the water wheel.

It had come loose from the broken rusty iron bar (shaft) that had connected it to the grinding wheel inside the mill, so Izzzzzabela wriggled her way up the water wheel and over the broken bit and slithered through the hole in the wall into the old mill and stopped.

She wrapped herself round the iron bar that was still in place, fixed to a large flat, wheel-shaped piece of machinery inside a huge room.

Izzzzzabela saw that the flock of sheep were huddled together in the far corner of the room. A pile of grass and a small water trough was next to them but none of them were eating or drinking.

They were all looking at the sheepdog which sat staring at them with a glaring look in its eyes.

The sheep kept shuffling, pushing against each other,

trying to get as far away as possible from the dog, bleating in terror, whenever it growled if one of them got near to it.

The two humans were sitting on old boxes. One was speaking on a mobile phone, and the other was sharpening a big knife with a small stone.

Izzzzzabela decided that she had seen enough, so she turned and wriggled her way back the way she had come and slithered as fast as she could towards the bridge to tell the others what she had seen.

'Well,' said Bulfrey, a while later, as they all lay amid a patch of tall bracken and some bushes by the bridge. It made a good place to hide.

'I think the first thing is, how do we get the sheepdog away from the flock? The humans wouldn't be able to move them would they? I mean not properly. Isn't that right, Eulia?'

Eulia nodded her head.

'Yes, and because they have been so afraid for such a long time, even a sheepdog would find it hard to move them to where they should go.'

'What if I go up to the old mill doors and make some noises,' said Swerlie-Wherlie. 'They might send the dog out to chase me away.'

Then he said, 'Err, I don't know what would happen then. It was a stupid idea anyway.'

'Now, now, don't say that,' said Bulfrey kindly. 'It is a good idea but we need a bit more help to make it work. Someone to make sure you don't get hurt while you are doing it, Swerlie-Wherlie.'

'Yes, but who?' he asked, 'There's no one else here.'

'I say,' a voice called from above them. 'Is this a party. Can anyone join?'

Circling just over them was Barney the owl.

Izzzzzabela hissed angrily when she saw him.

Swerlie-Wherlie hurriedly spoke up.

'Oh, hi Barney, you know everybody, especially Izzzzzabela, don't you and it's not a party as such but if you like come down and join us. We could use some help.'

Izzzzzabela hissed again when she heard this but kept still.

Barney circled around again and swooped down to a nearby tree branch looking anxiously at Izzzzzabela.

Swerlie-Wherlie was desperate to keep the peace between Barney and Izzzzzabela.

'Now that Barney knows that Izzzzzabela is my friend, I think he has something to say to her, don't you Barney?'

Barney hopped from one taloned foot to the other in embarrassment.

'Err, I..., err...'

He blinked his large eyes several times.

'I'm sss sorry I picked you up by mistake the other day and I'm glad you weren't hurt when you fell ... when I dropped you in the farmyard pond.'

'Well I suppose anyone can make mistakes,' said Izzzzzabela in a more friendly voice.

'I hope we can become friends too Barney. What do you say?'

Phew, thought Barney, *I don't deserve this. I don't have many friends but Izzzzzabela, wow.*

'Sure, I'd like to be to be your friend.'

'Good,' said Bulfrey.

'Now that's sorted. Tell Barney about our problem.'

Barney listened to the story and immediately offered to help Swerlie-Wherlie when he was ready to go to the mill and tease the sheepdog into coming outside.

So as soon as Bulfrey said that they had no time to waste, Swerlie-Wherlie set off for the mill doors, with Barney flying overhead.

Using the dried up stream bed as cover, Swerlie-Wherlie crept along until he was near the big lorry, still making lots of black smoke from its noisy engine.

Climbing up the banking of the old stream bed, he crept towards the large double doors, the shiny chain now hanging from one door handle and he saw that they were partly open and he could hear the poor sheep inside bleating. They were still very frightened.

Taking a big breath, *just like Cockie the cockerel would have done,* he thought with a smile, he began to grunt and oink as loudly as he could, before running to hide under the noisy lorry.

A few moments later the sheepdog ran out barking furiously, then stopped and looked around puzzled.

Then it saw Swerlie-Wherlie under the lorry and with bared teeth, rushed at him.

Oh no, thought Swerlie-Wherlie, *as he scrambled out from under the lorry. What do I do now?*

The big sheepdog bounded up, growling fiercely.

'You're for it now piglet.'

Then out of the sky came a flash of feathers and the screech of an owl.

Barney had arrived in the nick of time.

Feet first, his sharp talons nipped the sheepdog on his back before he swooped upwards and flipped in the air to attack again.

The sheepdog howled, more in shock than pain and turned to run back into the old mill.

Barney was ready for that. He flew down across the front of the big doors, hooting loudly.

The sheepdog gave a yelp and turned back to the lorry.

With a twitch of his wings, Barney spun round and dived at the sheepdog again.

The way to the lorry was blocked, so the now panicky sheepdog ran down to the dried up stream bed.

Barney flew after him, hooting for all he was worth.

The sheepdog got the shock of his life when racing up the far bank of the old stream he saw the huge shape of Bulfrey towering above him.

Bulfrey gave a huge bellow when he saw the sheepdog.

It echoed all around the mill yard and the sheepdog skidded to a halt, not knowing which way to go.

Barney swooped down again, still hooting loudly and the sheepdog scrambled madly through the nearest hedge and ran onto the lane, yelping for help.

A few more dives and hoots from Barney and the sheepdog decided that it had had enough and it began to run down the lane away from the old mill and the sheep.

Barney made sure that it didn't come back.

By now the humans in the old mill knew that something was wrong.

One of them had got into the lorry and was turning it around whilst the other kept guard by the big doors, making sure no sheep could escape.

Just then, Swerlie-Wherlie came back, running up to them as fast as his tiny trotters could go. He was panting heavily from his effort.

'W.... We need to stop them from leaving the mill yard,' he gasped.

'What do you think Bulfrey?'

'I think you're right.'

And Bulfrey turned to Buttercup and Daisy, who had been patiently waiting to help all this time.

'Would you two go and lie down in the gateway to the old mill,' he asked them.

'It will give me more time to think of a better way of stopping their lorry from leaving.'

Buttercup and Daisy nodded, and went off straight away towards the gate.

Then Izzzzzabela, who had climbed a nearby tree to keep a look out since Barney was still chasing the sheepdog, came back with the news that the humans were loading the flock onto the lorry without the sheepdog.

Poor Eulia was really upset when she heard this.

'Come on,' Swerlie-Wherlie said urgently to Bulfrey.

'Let's get closer and see if there is a way of stopping them getting away with the flock.'

So they went through the thickest bushes and trees towards the water wheel side of the mill, hoping that they wouldn't be seen. But the bad humans were too busy with the flock to notice them.

The water wheel was huge but Swerlie-Wherlie noticed a few things about it.

It was not fixed to the wall because the iron bar had rusted away in places and the mill was built on a slope. It had to be because the water in the stream flowed downhill and this is what turned the big wheel.

'Bulfrey, Bulfrey, look, the big wheel is loose,' he said excitedly.

'Do you think you can push it?'

'Push it. Of course I could push it. Why?'

'Well, do you think Daisy and Buttercup can stop that big lorry?'

'Err, for a short time, maybe,' Bulfrey said thoughtfully. 'But they could be injured too.'

Bulfrey looked closely at Swerlie-Wherlie and then said quietly, 'What do you want me to do?'

Suddenly, Swerlie-Wherlie felt afraid.

What if he was not doing the right thing. All-sorts of things might go wrong.

Then the lorry's engine began to get louder.

'They must be getting ready to leave,' shouted Swerlie-Wherlie.

'Do it now Bulfrey,' he cried.

'Do it now!'

Bulfrey went to the far side of the water wheel.

He was standing in the dry stream bed and put his big shoulder against the water wheel and pushed.

There was a loud creaking noise and the water wheel rocked forward and then rolled back.

'Harder, Bulfrey, harder,' Swerlie-Wherlie shouted as loud as he could.

'You can do it – you must.'

Then he groaned.

'Oh no! I think the lorry is moving. You can do it; you're the strongest bull in the world.'

Bulfrey took a big, big breath and pushed.

The water wheel rolled forward and Bulfrey pushed again.

It began to roll more quickly.

The steep slope now made the wheel roll faster and faster

as it went down the middle of the old dried up stream bed.

'It's going to miss the gate!'

Swerlie-Wherlie cried out in a disappointed voice.

'We've failed.'

Then Bulfrey suddenly bellowed.

'Daisy, Buttercup, get away from the gate. Get away now!'

The clatter of the rolling water wheel suddenly changed.

A loud thump was followed by a great big crash.

Daisy told them later that the big wheel had hit a rock just before the gate.

This had changed its course and it fell across the gateway just where she and Buttercup had been lying a moment before, completely blocking the way out from the mill yard.

The driver of the lorry had to stop very quickly to avoid crashing into the wrecked water wheel that now barred their way out of the old mill yard.

The two of them got out of the lorry and ran back to the old mill, leaving the terrified flock trapped in the back of it, bleating for help.

'You go and see where those humans are going, Swerlie-Wherlie. I have to get the flock out of that lorry, before anything else goes wrong,' Bulfrey said urgently, before he hurried away.

Swerlie-Wherlie nodded and went to the corner of the old mill and carefully had a look.

The two humans had just crossed the mill yard and were trying to open the big doors.

'You had the key to the padlock,' one was saying.

'No I didn't, you had it and now we're stuck. The two scooters are now locked inside. What are we to do?'

58

Swerlie-Wherlie happened to knock a stone with one of his trotters and the humans stopped arguing.

'Well, well, look what the farmer's brought us,' said one.

'A nice little piglet. Maybe the night hasn't been wasted after all.'

Swerlie-Wherlie felt very scared. He didn't want to be caught by these humans.

Then one of them screamed and pointed.

'Look, look an adder.'

And they both turned and ran round the corner of the old mill.

59

A moment later there was the sound of breaking wood and a cry of pain that seemed to echo.

'Why did they run away,' hissed Izzzzzabela, 'I'm not an adder (A poisonous snake). I'm a grass snake.'

'Never mind,' said a relieved piglet. 'Talk about saving my bacon. Let's go and see what all that noise was.'

They got quite a shock when they saw what had happened. The two humans had run over the top of an old well. The wooden covering had caved in and they had fallen down two or three metres onto a layer of thick mud. The well was just deep enough to stop them climbing out by themselves.

'I think they can stay here for a bit, don't you Izzzzzabela. They won't be going anywhere for a while. Let's go and see what Bulfrey's been up to, shall we.'

They found that Bulfrey had to head butt the rear door of the lorry several times before it fell down as a ramp so that the flock could all walk down safely to be met by a tearful Eulia.

'My darlings, my darlings. You are all safe, thanks to Bulfrey, Swerlie-Wherlie, Izzzzzabela and Barney,' who happened to be flying above them just then.

'I know you are all tired and hungry, but give a cheer for them,' she said to her flock.

But the flock was still confused with what had happened to them and they shouted.

'Baaaaaney, Baaaaaney, Baaaaaney.'

High above them Barney the owl blushed. He never knew that he had that many friends.

Just then Farmer Blox arrived with two of his men.

They were looking for Bulfrey and his two friends, Daisy and Buttercup.

Then he noticed the flock of sheep and the big lorry.

He took out his mobile and made a call, then asked his men to have a look around.

They soon heard the two bad men in the well shouting for help. They thought that since they were not really hurt, they could wait for the police to deal with them.

Swerlie-Wherlie and Izzzzzabela had said a hurried goodbye to Bulfrey and Eulia and had quietly left the old mill yard unnoticed by Farmer Blox.

After a while, as they came to the acorn tree, Izzzzzabela said that she had to see a friend and so she said bye to Swerlie-Wherlie and hoped that the next time they met it would be less hectic.

'Me too,' he replied but she had gone.

When Swerlie-Wherlie reached the farmyard. It was so quiet.

Just like this morning, he thought.

Then Cockie came into view.

'Do you know what?' he said sharply to Swerlie-Wherlie, 'Barney has just told me that he saved a whole flock of sheep from certain doom. I sometimes wonder Swerlie-Wherlie, whatever will he say next. He's not going to pull the wool over my eyes, I can tell you.'

Then he asked.

'Have you ever heard this sung so well, and he took a deep breath.'

'Cockadoodle Doooooo!'

'Sorry Cockie,' said Swerlie-Wherlie with a smile and his ears still ringing.

'Got to run.'

He went towards the sty-pen.

And then he began to trot more quickly as he heard familiar voices.

'Hey, that's my place'

'No it isn't, it's mine.'

It's nice to be home, he thought.

*****

Swerlie-Wherlie
and Butts the Goat

'Quaaaack. Quaaaack.'

'Quaaaack. Quaaaack.'

The row from the duck pond stopped Swerlie-Wherlie just as he reached Farmer Blox's farmyard gate.

Looking round, he saw the farm cat, Scratch, crouched down by the edge of the duck pond. He was trying to reach a little duckling sitting on a small rock.

A big father drake, flapping wings spread wide, was trying to get between them. Three other ducks, swimming in the middle of the pond added to the noise, hoping to scare Scratch away.

'What do you think you are doing, Scratch.'

Striding out from behind the tractor, Cockie the cockerel called out. Then he said, 'Stop it now or I will get very cross with you.'

Scratch looked across at Cockie and slowly stood up and stretched his legs, before saying, 'I was only having a bit of fun Cockie. There's not much to do round here.'

'Fun! Fun,' squawked Cockie.

'Just look at poor little Donald. He's scared to death, poor thing.'

Scratch didn't hear. He had already scooted off. He had just remembered that it must be near milking time and he ran as quickly as he could to the milking shed. Farmer Blox always spilt some milk and he wasn't going to miss that.

Little Donald had by now jumped into the pond and had paddled over to the drake, his Uncle Qwacks, who had calmed down when Cockie had told off Scratch.

After making sure that little Donald was all right, they both swam over to the other ducks and then they all waddled out of the pond one after the other.

Something about cats not being allowed in the farmyard could just be heard as they went round the corner of the old barn.

Swerlie-Wherlie was very impressed by the way Cockie had stopped Scratch from teasing little Donald.

It didn't last.

Cockie was well known in the farmyard for being bossy and bad-tempered and his mood changed as soon as he saw Swerlie-Wherlie.

'I say,' he called crossly.

'Barney (the owl), told me that Farmer Blox had given all of you who helped rescue that flock of sheep from being stolen the other day, extra feed as a reward.'

Cockie stared at Swerlie-Wherlie with his beady eyes and went on.

'It's not fair. As a possible new member of the Poultry Fowl Club Choir, I need extra feed so that my voice is strong and full of vigour. You know, something like this.'

Taking a deep breath, he let go.

'Cockadoodle Doooooo!'

'Cockadoodle Doooooo!'

Swerlie-Wherlie, jumped back his ears ringing.

'Wow, that was great,' he said politely.

Then twisting round, he shouted, 'Sorry Cockie but I've just remembered something,' before running off down the lane.

It was quite a while before he stopped running and then found out he was in a new place.

He had never come this far before.

Passing the old mill where he and Bulfrey the bull and his other friends had saved the sheep flock, he had kept going until he was too tired to trot.

The lane had come to a dead end, just before a big hole in the hillside.

It was an old quarry.

(A place where building stones are got from the ground).

After a short rest, Swerlie-Wherlie decided to explore.

A steep narrow path led down one side of the quarry.

It zig-zagged to and fro as he went further down and then he slipped.

Head over trotters he fell over the edge of the path and before he could squeal for help his body was suddenly jerked to a halt by the branches of small tree growing on the hillside.

He was safe but stuck.

'I say, do you need any help?'

The voice came from below.

Swerlie-Wherlie looked down and saw a goat, not much older than himself. It had a wispy beard and two small horns.

'I'm Butts, by the way. We don't get many piglets down here. Are you lost?'

'Err, sort of,' Swerlie-Wherlie said, careful not to shake the tree branches too much as he spoke.

He told Butts his name and how he had run all the way from Blox farm.

'Oh, I know that farm,' said Butts.

'It's not a very friendly place is it? The last time I was there I was nearly shot by the farmer. I think he thought I was a fox. Then another time a big owl zoomed past me as though his tail feathers were on fire. Nearly knocked me over he did. I'm sure he had a snake in his talons as well. Then there is that big cockerel. He always tells me to clear off or else I'll get it. He never says what it is I'll get. Funny that.'

Swerlie-Wherlie remembered those things too. He had never seen Butts though. There had been too much going on anyway.

'It's not that bad really. You must have come at the wrong times,' he said, trying to make it sound better than it seemed to Butts.

'If you say so,' Butts said, in a voice that sounded as though he didn't believe him.

'I'll climb up to you and then see how to get you out of that tree.'

Make it quick, thought Swerlie-Wherlie to himself. A small twig was sticking into his ribs and it was making him sore.

Soon the clack of small hooves on the path nearest to Swerlie-Wherlie, told him Butts was near.

'It's not too bad,' said Butts.

68

'Put your two back trotters a bit further down and push through the gap in the branch next to your head.'

It worked.

Swerlie-Wherlie was able to scramble up through the branches and onto the path.

'Ooh, that's better. Thanks a million Butts. I don't think I could have managed it on my own.'

Then he lay down on a patch of grass to get his breath back.

It had been a nasty shock and he was really glad that Butts had come along and helped him.

Butts lay down as well next to Swerlie-Wherlie and waited until he was ready to go on.

'I think you should follow me down this path. I know it very well. My friends and I play here quite often. In fact if you are feeling better, I could show you one of my secret places. It's not too far from here.'

Swerlie-Wherlie's ears pricked up.

A secret place.

He couldn't wait.

The path became very narrow. Butts didn't seem to mind as they went slowly along the sides of the big quarry, as though the big drop to the bottom wasn't there.

Swerlie-Wherlie wasn't so sure.

He stopped.

Maybe, he thought, *it isn't a good idea after all to visit Butt's secret place.*

He took a big breath and went on, even more slowly this time, glad that his small trotters meant that he had no trouble keeping on the path, though the big drop to the bottom of the quarry still scared him.

'You're doing all right, so far,' said Butts, as they reached a part of the path that had fallen away.

'This bit is tricky but I'm sure you'll manage. We have to jump over this little gap.'

'Gap. What gap?'

Swerlie-Wherlie tried to see what Butts was talking about.

Butts was in the way, so he couldn't. Not for long though.

Butts crouched down a little and suddenly jumped over the gap, landing safely on the other side.

'See. Dead easy,' he called out.

'Come on, Swerlie-Wherlie. You can do it.'

'Err, I'm not that good at jumping. My legs are not as long as yours you know.'

And he looked again at the gap and shivered.

Then he looked down, wishing that he hadn't. It was a long, long way to the bottom. I bet there is a horrible pool down there as well, he thought. (Piglets don't like being in deep water).

Butts called out to him. He wanted to help.

'If you keep thinking about it, you won't do it. Oh, another thing. Do you think you can turn round safely on this tiny path. I couldn't.'

Swerlie-Wherlie took a quick look behind him and knew that Butts was right. He had to jump.

So, moving back a little, he crossed his twirly tail for luck and rushing forward, jumped.

'There, that wasn't too bad was it,' said Butts over his shoulder. Even he couldn't turn round just here on the narrow path.

'Anyway, we're almost there now. Come on,' he said, leading the way.

The path went round a curve in the side of the quarry and passed a small cave.

'Here we are,' said Butts as he went towards the narrow entrance of the cave.

It was hard to see inside the cave and at the back it became a passage, so dark that Swerlie-Wherlie couldn't see a thing.

'Don't worry,' Butts voice echoed in the passage, 'You will be able to see soon. Just a few more steps.'

Swerlie-Wherlie hoped he was right. He had knocked his front two trotters several times against stones sticking up from the floor because he couldn't see them and they were beginning to hurt.

Then, as he followed the sound of Butts' hooves, he saw a light.

A human light fixed to the passage wall flickered, dimmed then got brighter.

'I told you we would be able to see, didn't I,' Butts said cheerfully.

'Yes, but the light was put there by humans, wasn't it?'

'Well I suppose it was. So what.'

'What if they were put there by bad humans? We might get caught.'

Just like the sheep flock, thought Swerlie-Wherlie.

'Don't be silly,' said Butts with a laugh.

'There are no humans here. I've been here lots of times and ......'

Butts stopped so suddenly that Swerlie-Wherlie bumped into him.

'Look, over there. Look,' cried Butts excitedly.

'What is it?'

The passage went into a chamber (a small room). Some old boxes were stacked against one of the walls and two small wooden doors, both closed, were on the other side. Another light shone from the roof of the chamber this time not so bright, but they could just see the entrance to another passage on the far side of it.

'I've never seen these before. I wonder what they are for,' he said, going closer for a look.

A scuffling noise behind one of the doors, made him stop.

He heard a sort of bark and then a whine.

'That sounds like a dog,' said Swerlie-Wherlie.

'Why would a dog be in here?'

At the sound of their voices, the door shook as something banged it.

'Let me out. Let me out,' a weak voice called.

'Hey, that sounds like Shep, Farmer Blox's sheepdog,' cried Swerlie-Wherlie in amazement.

'Shep, Shep, is that you in there? It's me, Swerlie-Wherlie, with my friend Butts.'

Nothing happened for a moment, and then the voice said.

'Swerlie-Wherlie, what are you doing in here? Don't you know it's dangerous for us animals?'

'What do you mean, Shep?'

(For it was Shep locked in behind the door).

'Some humans took me away from the farm. I heard one say that Farmer Blox will never win a sheepdog trial again once I'm sorted.'

'That sounds bad,' said Butts.

'We'll try and get you out as quick as we can.'

'I hope so. It's horrible in here. There's not enough room to swing a cat and it's dark. I can't see anything.'

A sudden sound from the passage behind him made Butts jump and he looked round and saw a moving shadow.

'Run, Swerlie-Wherlie. Run.'

He shouted in alarm.

'The bad humans are coming.'

There was only one way to go and Swerlie-Wherlie ran towards the other passage as fast as his little trotters would let him.

Butts, with his longer legs kept up easily and was soon in front as they both raced along the new passage.

It was lit with a few dim lights, so they could see where they were going, until Butts yelled out.

'Stop! Stop!'

Too late.

As Butts slowed down, Swerlie-Wherlie ran into him and knocked him over.

Right over the edge of a big crack, which lay across the passage floor.

It was big enough for Butts to fall into, with poor Swerlie-Wherlie following, head over trotters.

Lucky for them it was a short fall.

They landed on a sandy slope and they skidded and rolled down a bit more, tangled up with each other, until they reached the bottom.

'Argh,' said Butts, spitting out a mouthful of sand.

'Are you okay?'

Swerlie-Wherlie spluttered, and whispered, 'I think so,' as he pulled away from one of Butts' legs which was lying across his back.

'Where are we?'

Butts stood up and looked around.

They were in a small tunnel where part of the roof had collapsed a long time ago.

Before they could decide what to do, a human voice shouted. It echoed all around the underground passages.

'I can't see them. I think they fell down into the bottom chamber. They'll never get out of there. We may as well go back. Don't forget we have to take that sheepdog away tomorrow.'

Then.

'Okay, I'm coming.'

'Did you hear that,' Swerlie-Wherlie said in a worried voice.

'Poor Shep is going to be taken away. What can we do?'

Butts had no idea what to do and he was thinking that they really needed some help to get out of the tunnel they were trapped in.

'Well,' he said, trying to be cheerful, 'Let's explore this tunnel. Have you noticed, Swerlie-Wherlie, that there are some little lights on down here. The humans must have forgotten to turn them off.'

That really cheered Swerlie-Wherlie up.

He was actually a bit afraid of being too long in the dark.

'Great,' he said.

'Which way do you think we should go.'

'Err, what about that way,' said Butts, pointing his small horns to where the passage sloped down.

'Maybe that way leads to the bottom of the quarry.'

'All right then you go first. You're the biggest.'

So Butts led the way through the twisting tunnel.

It was easy at first, and then the floor began to get steeper, and steeper.

'I say Butts. Have you noticed that we are walking uphill.'

Butts stopped and looked at the floor. It was steeper in front of him.

'You know, you are right. I never noticed, except that I am getting more tired.'

'I think we're lost,' said Swerlie-Wherlie in a worried voice and he sat down with a little thump, on the sandy floor.

'And I need a drink and soon. My trotters are aching like mad.'

'My hooves too,' agreed Butts as he lay down besides Swerlie-Wherlie.

The sound of a swishing noise woke him.

He had drifted off to sleep, just like Swerlie-Wherlie who was now gently snorting away in a deep dream, his twirly tail twitching in time to the snorts.

Butts looked across the sandy floor of the tunnel and jerked upright with a start.

The swishing noise was being made by a snake.

It was slithering around and around in the sand, making a circle in front of Swerlie-Wherlie.

'Wake up! Hey! Swerlie-Wherlie! Wake up! We're being attacked by snakes.'

With the biggest snort, Swerlie-Wherlie woke up and saw a snake.

'Oh hello, Izzzzzabella,' he said quietly.

'What are you doing here?'

'Well, I was taking a short cut through these old passages, to see my best friend Twisteen, when I felt the vibration of something falling into this tunnel.

You did know that snakes can feel the ground shake far and away much better than most animals, don't you. Anyway, It took me quite a while to get here to see what it was. It was a big surprise to find both of you asleep.

So I sort of slithered around until you woke,' Izzzzzabella added, as she formed her body into a coil.

Her head was now high enough to look at them easily.

Swerlie-Wherlie sat up and then said. 'That's Butts over there, trying to hide in that hole in the wall. Come out, Butts,' he called.

'This is one of my friends. She won't bite.'

76

'I don't bite. I'm a grass-snake,' hissed Izzzzzabella proudly.

Butts slowly left the hole in the wall.

It wouldn't have hidden a large rabbit let alone a young goat, and he stood nervously next to Swerlie-Wherlie.

'As I was saying,' Swerlie-Wherlie went on, 'We have a problem that you might help us with, Izzzzzabella.'

When Swerlie-Wherlie had finished telling her about Shep and how he had to be rescued soon, Izzzzzabella agreed to help.

'I know this place very well,' she hissed.

'My friend Twisteen's family have lived round here for ages. She once told me that one of her great, great, great granddads, saw the humans make this big hole in the ground, using little sticks that made big bangs that broke the rock into smaller pieces.

Twisteen showed me the two little rooms they kept the little sticks in. You must have passed them.....'

'Hey.'

Swerlie-Wherlie interrupted Izzzzzabella with a shout.

'I bet that's where Shep is. You remember don't you, Butts. Those two little doors and Shep was in there wasn't he?'

Butts nodded in agreement.

Swerlie-Wherlie became very excited.

'Is there another way to those little rooms, Izzzzzabela,' he asked hoping there would be.

'Well, this passage does go up towards the next level. You were actually going back to a place near to where the little doors are. The problem is fallen stones have blocked the passage. I can wriggle through but ....'

Izzzzzabella stopped hissing.

Nobody said anything for a while.

They were thinking hard.

Then Swerlie-Wherlie looked over at them and said urgently.

'We have to try and save Shep.'

'Let's go and have a look. You never know, it might not be as bad as Izzzzzabella says,' said Butts hopefully.

They all looked at each other and then Izzzzzabella hissed, 'Follow me.'

She wriggled along the passage quite quickly, knowing exactly where to go and the other two were soon puffing and blowing, trying to keep up.

It was made worse because they were still going higher and higher.

Then Izzzzzabella stopped in front of a pile of fallen rocks and stones, which reached right up to the roof of the passage.

Swerlie-Wherlie groaned in disappointment.

'We'll never get through that lot in a million years.'

'Well. There is one thing I remember about going through this pile of stones,' Izzzzzabella hissed.

'It didn't take me long to get through.'

Swerlie-Wherlie suddenly had an idea, then thought it was no good. It seemed a bit stupid.

Still .....

'I say, you two,' he said excitedly.

'What do you think of this.'

And he told them.

Izzzzzabella had shown Butts where she had wriggled through the pile of rocks.

It was just about head high for him and he could see the small hole she had used before.

Then he noticed the rock on the top of the hole was sticking out a bit and it seemed to wobble as they looked at it.

'I think it's worth a go,' said Butts.

'It's dangerous but I'll do it. Stand well back, you two.'

When they had moved safely back down the passage, Butts put his head down and charged the rock above the hole.

Crash!

His two horns banged into the rock and knocked the bit sticking out sideways.

This caused the rock above it to fall, and then another.

Then the whole wall of rocks and stones began to fall to the floor.

'Butts,' yelled Swerlie-Wherlie as loud as he could.

'Get out of the way. Get out of the way. You'll get buried. Oh no, he's gone.'

A cloud of dust hid Butts from view and Swerlie-Wherlie and Izzzzzabella feared the worst as they coughed and spluttered in it.

The dust soon settled and what a surprise they got.

Butts stood on a pile of rocks, covered in dust but smiling with pride. He had done it and all by himself.

He looked down and said, 'We goats can climb and jump better than most other animals. As the rocks began to fall I just jumped from one to the other until I reached the top. Oh, by the way, the passage is open now. Your idea worked a treat, Swerlie-Wherlie.'

It was a bit awkward for Swerlie-Wherlie, with his small legs, to climb over the new, smaller pile of rocks but he made it and they soon reached the place where Shep was locked in.

'Shep, Shep.'

There was no answer.

'Call again,' said Butts.

'All right.'

And Swerlie-Wherlie banged the small door with one of his trotters and shouted.

'Shep are you in there. It's me.'

'Maybe he's asleep,' hissed Izzzzzabella.

'Not with that row,' said Butts.

'I'm going to open the door. Stand back.'

He went to the other side of the passage and ran at the small door, his head low, horns at the ready.

Bang!

Butts staggered back and sat down, shaking his head. Then he looked up.

The little door was open.

But Shep was gone.

'The humans must have come early and taken him away,' said a disappointed Swerlie-Wherlie.

He was upset because they had not got there soon enough.

Izzzzzabella slithered across the floor and made a body coil before hissing. 'I think they might have taken Shep down to the bottom of the quarry. Sometimes I have seen one of those moving things with no legs, sitting there.'

'Oh, you mean a lorry,' said Swerlie-Wherlie.

He had seen many of those in Farmer Blox's farmyard.

'Yes, if that's what you call them. There is a way out of the quarry that goes to a lane.'

'We have to hurry then, before they take Shep away,' said Butts.

'Is there a quicker way down that you can show us?' he asked Izzzzzabella.

'Well,' she hissed, 'If you want a quick way, I know of a funny passage. It is a lot smaller than this one and it is very steep. I don't think you will like it.'

'If it gets us to the bottom of the quarry quickly, let's go,' Swerlie-Wherlie said in a fierce voice.

'We still have to find Shep.'

So Izzzzzabella led them along the passage until they came to small hole in the wall.

'This is the place,' she hissed.

It was just big enough for Butts to squeeze into and he noticed that it sloped down a lot.

Just as Izzzzzabella had said.

The floor was sandy and he found it easy to slide down.

'Come on, Swerlie-Wherlie.' he shouted, as he disappeared.

'Just dig your trotters in the sand and you won't go too fast.'

Swerlie-Wherlie didn't like going into the dark tunnel, so crossing his twirly tail for luck, he followed Butts head first, his front trotters pressed gently in the sand and then he gave a push.

Izzzzzabella waited a few moments and then slithered after him. She had been down here a few times before and so wasn't worried about it.

Oh no, she thought, *I forgot to tell them about the pool.*

Splash!

'What the ....'

Butts had shot out of the tunnel and landed in the big pool. It was deep and he started to sink.

Water entered his mouth and he began to splutter as he swallowed some of it.

The shock of the cold water made him paddle his legs like mad and this made him rise to the surface of the pool. He had just taken a big breath of fresh air when....

'Look out!'

Swerlie-Wherlie cried out in alarm as he saw Butts head suddenly appear out of the water, fortunately just missing him.

Swerlie-Wherlie sank down and then seemed to bounce back to the surface, floating like a baby duckling that had just fallen off its parents back.

Before he could say or do anything, he saw Izzzzzabella fly like an arrow through the air and plunge into the water, before popping up without any trouble and wiggle her way to the edge of the pool.

Butts, his sodden coat making him feel much heavier, called out to Swerlie-Wherlie.

'Last one to Izzzzzabella is a ...' he spluttered.

He had swallowed some water and Swerlie-Wherlie never found out what he had meant to say.

A pile of dry grass and bracken soon dried them off, though of course, Izzzzzabella didn't need to, being a reptile.

The pool had been made a long time ago when a wall of rocks and tree logs had been built across the quarry near to the place where a stream fell as a waterfall down one side of its steep walls.

As Swerlie-Wherlie led the way past the end of the pool, he stopped to look at some of the logs that were rotten and where a jet of water was squirting out from between them.

It reminded him of the water pipe Farmer Blox used when he cleaned the farmyard.

'Come on,' Butts called out urgently.

'Shep could have been taken away by now.'

Before Swerlie-Wherlie could say anything, Izzzzzabella came wriggling up to them and hissed, 'I have just seen Shep being put in the back of that thing you call a lorry.'

A worried Swerlie-Wherlie ran forward with Izzzzzabella, along an old grassy track to where the ground dipped down into a hollow.

Hiding behind a bush, they saw Shep pulling on a piece rope, which tied him to the back of the driving cab of a small lorry.

The lorry was stuck, a back wheel had fallen into a hole and was spinning so fast, that smoke was coming from the tyre, as the driver tried to get free.

The other human was pushing the lorry from the back. He was coughing loudly because of the black smoke coming from the spinning tyre.

'Will you keep watch while I go and tell Butts of an idea that might help us rescue Shep,' Swerlie-Wherlie asked.

Izzzzzabella hissed back.

'All right.'

So he rushed back, shouting, 'Butts, Butts. Come with me quick.'

'What's going on?' Butts asked.

'There is only one way we can stop them getting away with Shep and you are the only one who can do it,' Swerlie-Wherlie said excitedly.

'Do what?' said Butts a bit confused.

'Come on. There's no time to waste. Follow me to the pool. I'll show you the place.'

Butts followed Swerlie-Wherlie to the big wall of rocks and logs that made the big pool.

'Look, can you see that rotten log sticking out, just where the water is squirting out.'

Butts nodded.

Of course he could see it and it was splashing him as well, so he moved backwards a bit.

'So,' he asked.

'What do I have to do?'

Swerlie-Wherlie was nearly jumping up and down with excitement.

'You have to bang it with your head, you know, like you did to that door in the passage. It's the only way to save Shep.'

'Well...'

Butts wasn't sure.

'Hurry!' urged Swerlie-Wherlie.

'We can't wait any longer.'

Butts moved right back as Swerlie-Wherlie moved to one side, keeping well out of his way.

Lowering his head, Butts took a deep breath.

He charged the pool wall and his hard curved horns bashed into the rotten log.

A big piece broke off and a great squirt of water shot out, soaking both of them.

'Run to this side,' Butts cried, as he shoved Swerlie-Wherlie as hard as he could away from the pool wall, which had now begun to crack.

More and more water squirted through.

Suddenly, the whole wall of rocks and logs gave way and a huge wave of water rushed down the track towards the hollow, carrying rocks and bits of logs with it.

The two humans heard the roar of rushing water.

The driver jumped out of the lorry just in time and ran after the other one towards the lane, shouting for him to wait.

The wave of water reached the lorry and swirled all around before it became deep enough to float it.

Then the lorry began to spin and poor Shep, howling in terror, desperately tried to pull free from the rope that kept him tied to it.

'What can we do?' shouted Swerlie-Wherlie.

'If the lorry sinks, Shep will drown.'

Butts nodded. He had noticed that there were lots of broken logs floating in the water and some were near the lorry.

'Keep back. The water is still rising and it's far too deep for you to do anything anyway,' he said.

Then .....

Before Swerlie-Wherlie could say something, Butts had jumped from the track onto the nearest log.

Hooves slipping, Butts leapt to another one, then another, just keeping his balance as he noticed that the lorry's back part was floating quite near.

'*So take a chance,*' Butts said to himself.

'*It's now or never.*'

And he jumped onto the back of it.

The lorry lurched to one side and began to sink.

Shep stopped pulling on the rope and whined at the thought that he would never be saved as the water began to splash round his paws.

A wet body suddenly pushed him over as Butts rushed to him and the rope that held him.

Goats eat all sorts of things and the rope was no problem for Butts. His sharp teeth bit through it in one big bite.

'Come on Shep. We have to jump now, the lorry is sinking fast.'

Shep couldn't believe it.

Where had Butts come from.

He didn't care.

With a quick, 'Thank you, Butts,' he jumped into the cold water.

Just in time, Butts followed Shep as the lorry sank, engine first, with the back part sticking up as the water sloshed over the rear wheels.

Shep was shaking his fur dry by the time Butts landed by the track where Swerlie-Wherlie and Izzzzzabella were anxiously waiting.

'Are you all right,' they called.

'Well apart from being soaking wet again, I'm okay,' said a relieved Butts.

'What about you Shep?'

'I could eat for a week. I've had nothing but some old biscuits and water for the last few days.'

He rubbed his neck with a paw where the rope had made it sore.

'How did you find me? I thought I would never get rescued.'

Before they could say anything, the sound of a motorcycle echoed round the quarry.

'I bet that's Farmer Blox coming for you Shep,' said Swerlie-Wherlie.

'So we'll get off, if that's all right and I'll tell you all about it later, okay.'

Shep nodded tiredly.

He was worn out and so he lay down to wait for Farmer Blox.

Butts led Swerlie-Wherlie and Izzzzzabella back into the quarry, past the now nearly empty pool and they began to slowly climb up the steep zig-zag path to the top.

When they got there, Butts said, 'I shall have to leave you here. I'm staying with my Uncle Billy and he will be wondering where I am.'

'Me too,' added Izzzzzabella.

'I have to see my friend Twisteen. Bye.'

Before Swerlie-Wherlie or Butts could say anything, she had gone.

Butts looked at Swerlie-Wherlie and said with a big smile.

'Careful how you go. You don't want to fall and get stuck again. Do you?'

'You bet,' replied Swerlie-Wherlie and waved a trotter goodbye, as Butts went on his way.

Whew, what a day it's been, he thought, as he went along the lane back to the farm.

As he went through the farm gate he heard a lot of noise and found the tractor surrounded by a crowd of ducks and hens.

Scratch was crouched on top of the tractor cabin, looking down and hissing angrily.

'One more time,' cried a voice.

It was Cockie and he began to lead the ducks and hens in a march round the tractor.

'And bring the roof down this time,' he called loudly as he took a deep breath.

'After three. And keep together,' he urged them.

'All right then. One... Two... Three.'

The chant began

Ducklings and Chicks, Love them to Bits.
'Ducklings and Chicks, Love them to Bits.
Scratch, Scratch has an itch.
'Ducklings and Chicks, Love them to Bits.
'Ducklings and Chicks, Love them to Bits.
Scratch, Scratch has an itch.

Cockie as ever, was the loudest!

The chanting stopped and Cockie called up to Scratch, still crouched on the tractor cab roof.

'We're just having a bit of fun. There's not much to do round here. Ha. Ha. Ha.'

Scratch looked down at them and wished he hadn't teased Donald the duckling that morning.

Swerlie-Wherlie turned from them and laughed all the way to his sty-pen.

****

90

The Author

Watercolour painting - Rita Clements Lee

ritaclementslee-artist.co.uk/

Printed in Poland
by Amazon Fulfillment
Poland Sp. z o.o., Wrocław

A Folktale Dominican

Lamar Coldwell

Rosen REAL READERS

Rosen Classroom™
New York

Our teacher reads us a folktale.
It is about a young girl named
Camila and a monster named
el Coco.

Camila lives in the Dominican
Republic. One day she
misbehaved. Her father asked her
to pick up her toys. She didn't
pick them up.

El Coco is a monster from Hispanic folktales. He comes and gets children who misbehave. He lives on a mountain inside of a cave.

He knows which children are
good and which children are bad.
He will come and get whomever
doesn't listen to their mom and
dad.

El Coco waits for children to go to bed. That is when he comes to get them.

El Coco creeps into town just before midnight. All is quiet, and everyone is in bed for the night.

El Coco goes to Camila's house. He slowly opens the door. He sees a large pile of toys on the floor.

El Coco steps over dolls. He steps over blocks. Then, he trips over a jack-in-the-box!

The jack-in-the-box opens. It makes a loud noise. El Coco runs out of the room. He hops over toys.

Camila learned a lesson the night el Coco was scared away. She listens to her parents and cleans up her toys every day.

Words to Know

el Coco

children

jack-in-the-box

misbehave

teacher

toys